ADAM WAS HERE

ADAM WAS HERE

A story about homelessness

by
Catherine Chambers

W
FRANKLIN WATTS
NEW YORK • LONDON • SYDNEY

First published in 1995 by Franklin Watts

This paperback edition published in 1998

Franklin Watts
96 Leonard Street
London EC2A 4RH

Franklin Watts Australia
14 Mars Road
Lane Cove
NSW 2066

Editor: Rosemary McCornick
Designer: Jason Anscomb
A CIP catalogue record for this book
is available from the British Library

ISBN 0 7496 3285 2 (pbk)
      0 7496 2025 0 (hbk)

Dewey Classification 306.9

Printed in Great Britain

Foreword

Few of us stop to ask ourselves "What is a home?" In fact most people take their home for granted. But each year nearly 140,000 households, mostly families with children, become homeless. On top of this, thousands of single people with nowhere to live end up on the streets. Because many of them have no legal right to help, they aren't included in the government's assessment of homelessness in this country.

No doubt hundreds of thousands of people, many of them very young, would give quite a different answer to the question "What is a home?" than most of us. At Centrepoint we have learnt from the young people that we work with that a home is somewhere secure, safe and happy.

Every year we see hundreds of children who have run away from home because they are frightened, lonely and vulnerable. Half the people we see are under 18 years old, and many of them have become homeless after years of uncertainty and stress.

Many of the young people who stay in our hostels and flats have seen their parents suffer as their homes are repossessed, have lived in terribly overcrowded houses and have had to move time and time again from one place to another, giving up schools, friends and homes.

In many families the strain of homelessness and poverty leads to rows and separation. There is a happy ending to this story with Adam and his family moving into a home of their own. But how much better it would be if children like Adam didn't have to face the hurt and damage of homelessness in the first place.

Nick Hardwick
Chief Executive, Centrepoint

One

Adam sat outside his house on the chipped white steps and looked out on to the busy street. Everything was cracking and crumbling - the paint on the front doors, the plaster on the walls, the pavement below. Even the autumn leaves looked crumpled and old as they blew along helplessly in the wind. But Adam loved that view — watching the changes.

He felt along the side of the top step with his fingers. As usual, a piece of loose brick pulled away, Adam stuck his hand inside this secret space and drew out an old army penknife. Mum never let him have the knife in the house. Very carefully, he carved into the white plaster on the wall behind him, 'Adam was here'.

"Move, lad!" said a young man carrying the kitchen table down the steps to a waiting van. Adam shifted just a little.

"I'm telling on you!" yelled Adam's sister as she dragged and bumped a large box full of all her special things.

"Why?" asked Adam.

"Because you've spoiled the wall," replied Lucy.

"Who cares? It's not our wall any more," said her brother.

"Where's your box, Adam?" asked Mum from

behind the front door.

"In my room." He sat for a minute, then looked up at his mother's tired face. "I'll go and get it," he said finally.

Adam put the piece of brick back into the hole and quietly slid his knife into the pocket of his jeans. He came back carrying an enormous box with posters and aeroplane wings sticking out of the top.

"Your box is too big," said Lucy. "Aunt Kath's and Uncle Chas's flat is too small for it."

"Shut up!" said Adam as he sat down next to her on the edge of the truck.

It was nearly time to go. Adam and Lucy watched their mother as she ran up and down the steps with the last few things: the vase from under the kitchen sink, a bucket and spade left out in the back yard — and a dog's lead. Lucy slipped the lead on to Devil's collar and hugged him tight. Devil's enormous fangs grinned up at her trustingly and his black, pointed ears twitched with hope that he was going for a walk.

"You're going to have a lovely time in the country," Lucy whispered to him. "I wish we were too."

Adam jumped from the van as the driver pulled down the door at the back. He stood and stared at two other men boarding up their home. The banging of nails echoed round the street as the house gradually lost its face. Great wooden sheets covered the windows. A piece of paper that said 'No mail, please' was stuck crookedly on the board that hid the door. A strong chain was wound round the front gate and the railings. A padlock was snapped shut. Finally, a 'For Sale' sign was planted in the small patch of earth by the front steps, shattering a rose bush still pink with late autumn blooms.

"Where are you going, Adam?" yelled a friend from across the street.

"To live with my aunt and uncle," said Adam.

"Will you still come to our school?" asked Ashok.

"Course. We're only going over there." Adam pointed to the top of some high-rise flats a few streets away.

Ashok shrugged. "OK, see you then," and he ran off, kicking stones into the gutter as he went.

The van gurgled to a start and then juddered as it struggled down the road. Adam, Lucy, Mum and Devil stood and watched.

"Come on," said Mum, "we've got to meet the van at the flats."

At the grey tower block, the removal men were already lifting boxes up concrete steps to Aunt Kath's flat. Adam and Lucy ran up to the third floor and leaned against the wall, out of breath. The cool September wind whistled through the open landing by Aunt Kath's door. They peeped round and ran towards the steamy light of the kitchen and the welcoming figure of their cheerful uncle.

"Uncle Chas!" cried Lucy, reaching her arms round his neck. "What are you doing here?"

"Being strangled!" he laughed. "No — took the

afternoon off — thought your aunt might need some help. Come on, I'll show you where you'll be sleeping."

Lucy was to share their parents' room. She jumped on to her bed and started unpacking her box of special things. Her mother's old doll with the hair falling out, a beloved Ted, her best painting, a stone with a fossil in it — well, maybe a fossil . . . Adam had a room all to himself. It was tiny, but he was glad to be on his own.

"Told you your box was too big!" Lucy's nose edged round Adam's door. Adam threw a paper aeroplane straight at her head.

"Come and say goodbye to Devil!" shouted Mum.

"And to my bike and my skateboard and my roller skates," muttered Adam.

Devil looked happy sitting beside the van driver. In fact, he looked rather smug. Lucy held Mum's hand tight as she waved goodbye.

"I hope Uncle Ed won't put Devil with our furniture in his barn," she said.

"Of course he won't," said Mum. "Devil will have the time of his life."

"Will we have the time of our lives, too?" asked Lucy. Mum hesitated.

"I don't know," she said. "That will really depend on us. But at least your dad won't be lying in hospital worrying about where we're going to live."

Adam's thoughts turned to his dad, and the months he had spent in hospital recovering from a road accident. He looked at Lucy's hopeful face and took a deep breath.

But the tiny flat quickly became their home. The balcony and the flights of stairs became a playground. The balcony was a mountain peak or a ship's crow's nest. It was a space station or a ski lift. And the children rolled marbles down the steps, tripping up the neighbours as they climbed the staircase. Mum took them out every day after school. And, for Adam and Lucy, playing in the park every day was almost as good as having their own garden.

Then one day, their happiness was complete.

"Dad! Dad!" shrieked Adam, as he opened the front door one late afternoon. "I didn't know you were coming home so soon!"

"Gently!" said Mum, as Adam and Lucy smothered their father with hugs. "Or he'll be back in hospital!"

That evening there were great celebrations. In the small kitchen, six chairs were squashed round the table. Glasses sparkled, candles flickered and the room became warm with steaming dishes and the sound of laughter. Dad and Mum would both get jobs. They'd get another house, even better than the last one. Oh yes, and Devil would come back! Everything would be all right now.

Next day Adam swung his bag happily as he walked into the classroom. There, pinned on the wall in front of a long table, he saw a huge painting of sky and grass.

"Today," said Mr Bannerman, their teacher, when they had all stopped fidgeting, "we're going to begin a project on our community. In a minute each of you will start to make a model of your own home. When you have finished, we'll put them on the table in front of the frieze. But before you begin, let's talk about it. Firstly, what d'you think a home is?"

"Please, sir, me! Me! I know what a home is! I know!" Thirty hands waved in the air and voices cawed like a hundred young crows.

"A home is a beautiful house . . . a big house with a long garden . . . it's a ground-floor flat with a proper back yard, I'm fed up with our tiny balcony! It's . . . it's . . ."

"A home is a sort of house," yelled a voice from the middle of the crowd of children. It was Adam. "A home is a happy place – where the whole family can live together!"

And by the end of the morning Adam had made his home. It was a tall box, painted grey like the flats, with graffiti on the walls and lots of tiny windows. Through a bigger window, on the third floor, yellow painted light shone on six smiling faces.

TWO

Adam would remember November for ever. Not for
the bleary, misty mornings. Not for the scent of
Christmas to come. He would remember breakfast time,
one grizzly Monday morning.

"It doesn't go there," said Aunt Kath to Mum, as
she put the milk in the fridge.

"What doesn't go where?" asked Mum.

"The milk, the milk — you know it doesn't go
there." Aunt Kath's voice was a little higher and a little
louder than usual.

Adam and Lucy put their spoons in their bowls
and sat very quietly

"But there's too much milk," said Mum, "so I put
some near the orange juice because —"

"I know there's too much," shouted Aunt Kath.
"There's too much of everything. Too much milk, too
much washing, too much dirt, too much noise — just too
much!"

There was complete silence. They could hear
muffled footsteps shuffling from the flat above and thin,
blurred voices. In a daze, Adam and Lucy stood up and
scraped their chairs on the tiled floor.

"Shhhh!" hissed Mum, and she guided them
quietly out of the kitchen.

After school that day, Adam and Lucy opened the door to the flat very slowly. Aunt Kath was in the kitchen, stirring some rice on the stove. Her face, flushed from the steam, she opened her arms and drew the children towards her in a big hug.

"I love you," she said, "and I'm really sorry about this morning."

Lucy put her hand on Aunt Kath's huge stomach.

"There's no room for us in your arms any more," she said. "When are you going to have your baby?"

"Soon," said Aunt Kath. "Very soon."

"Where's Mum and Dad?" asked Adam.

"Looking for work," Aunt Kath replied.

That evening Adam and Lucy ate their meal alone and in silence. Mum and Dad had not returned and Uncle Chas was still at work. Aunt Kath had gone to lie down.

"You'd better pick that bit of rice up from the floor," Adam told Lucy.

"It's not mine. Look! It's closer to your chair," replied Lucy.

"I saw you drop it," said Adam crossly "You never lean over your plate properly."

"I do, and anyway it looks like yesterday's rice," shouted Lucy, "so I'm not picking it up." She got up and smashed her chair hard into the table.

"Now look! You've trodden in it and it's going everywhere," yelled Adam. He grabbed Lucy's arm as she clawed at his pullover, screaming at him with rage . . .

They didn't hear the door open.

"What's all this?" thundered a voice that Adam and Lucy could hardly recognise. They swung round.

"Dad!"

There was silence. All they could hear was the faint echo of footsteps on the concrete stairs, way below.

"Is that Mum and Uncle Chas coming up?" asked Lucy. There was no reply.

"Did you and Mum find jobs?" Adam's voice shrank as he watched his father's angry eyes.

"Go to your rooms!" Dad said.

"Will we − ?" started Adam

"I said go to your rooms." He spoke in almost a whisper. But his anger, so very rare, filled Adam and Lucy with fear and shock. They walked quietly to their rooms. The front door opened again, and they could hear Dad talking to Mum and Uncle Chas.

Later, much later, when Lucy was fast asleep, Adam crept out of his room. He stood in the narrow hallway and peeped through the crack in the kitchen door. He watched his parents and his aunt and uncle as they finished their meal. They were talking, talking. Aunt Kath's arms waved around as she spoke, as they always did.

Uncle Chas seemed relaxed and cheerful, as he always was. Dad had his arm around Mum's shoulder. Everything was normal, quite normal.

Adam turned round to go back to his room, but stopped suddenly at a little hall table. A letter lay open, half of it tucked into an envelope addressed to the local Homeless Unit. Adam knew he should walk on, but could not stop himself from reading the part he could just manage to see. He recognised the writing. It was Aunt Kath's.

'Dear Madam,' the letter said.

'We have given shelter to my sister and her family since September 15th. But I am expecting a baby in a few weeks' time and we will need more space in our flat. So we can no longer give them a roof over their heads. Tomorrow. . .'

Adam could not see any more. But he did not want to. Stunned, he crept back into his room. How could Aunt Kath do this? And how could they all be sitting together so happily round the kitchen table?

Adam found it hard to get to sleep. He lay there watching his model aeroplane swinging from the ceiling. A cold moon shone on the proud Nighthawk's wings through a slit in the curtains. In the old house, there had been three aeroplanes. Each one had been strung slightly higher than the other, so that they looked as if they were soaring off together on an important mission. He'd had aeroplane posters stuck round the walls, too, in the old house. Mum said Aunt Kath wouldn't want a mess on her wallpaper, so he kept the posters in his box in a corner of the room. In the other house . . . Adam finally fell asleep.

Adam woke early the next morning. There was no one else up as he walked through the sitting room and unlocked the door to the balcony. He leaned his elbows on the railings and watched the council workers sweeping litter from the pavements. A tall man with a short, sharp stick was spearing empty cigarette boxes and crisp bags.

Adam turned his back on them and crouched down. He felt in his back pocket and drew out his penknife. On a piece of grey wall, close to the balcony floor, he scratched, 'Adam was here'.

When the rest of the family appeared, Adam smiled a bit more than usual. He didn't want anyone to know that he had discovered the letter. Mum and Dad looked tense, but Dad wasn't angry any more. They talked cheerfully at the breakfast table as they always did, planning for the future, hoping . . .

Adam threw himself into the classroom, glad that he didn't have to grin any longer. Glad that he could think about his lessons and not his problems. Glad that he was with people who knew nothing of his grey November . . .

"Mr Bannerman!" a sharp, shrill voice cut through the gentle hum of the children working. It was the school secretary, bustling towards the frieze. Mr Bannerman was sitting on the long table cutting out street names and shop signs.

"Yes, Mrs Haig," he said quietly,

"Is Adam Fox in this class?" she asked.

"Yes, he's sitting over there," and Mr Bannerman pointed towards Adam's table. "Why?"

"The Homeless Unit just want to check that he's real and that he comes to school here. It's amazing what some people will say just to get a house, you know. They'll even invent a few children." Mrs Haig strutted out, leaving a trail of perfume behind her.

The busy humming sound changed to whispering. All the other children had heard every word. Adam wanted to run, but where would he run to? Home? He laughed and choked and then cried to himself.

"Are you going homeless, Adam?" a girl's voice rang through the mumblings and mutterings. Adam said nothing.

"I went homeless last year," said the girl.

Adam raised his face slowly from his hands and looked round the classroom. The girl smiled . . . and Adam nodded his head in answer to her question but he couldn't quite manage to smile back.

Three

At the end of school, Adam spent a long time looking round the playground for Lucy. He never went home without her — he'd never dare! Just by the gate Mum's blue coat caught his eye. Adam ran towards her, thinking that something was wrong. Mum hardly ever met them from school these days. She was too busy trying to find a job.

"Everything all right?" he asked, even before he'd stopped running. "Where's Lucy? Oh, there you are. How was I supposed to find you, you stupid girl," Adam snapped.

"We've no time for bickering," Mum said. "Here, take your bag. I've packed just your most important things and I've got your clothes in this suitcase."

"Why? Where are we going?" asked Adam.

Mum put down the heavy suitcase and brushed the hair away from his forehead.

"Look," she said softly. "Kath and Chas have shared their home and been so good to us. But their baby's coming soon. And in any case, we've just got to get a place of our own — we all know that really, don't we?"

Adam thought of the letter.

"They've thrown us out, haven't they?" he said

angrily.

"It's not like that . . . " began Mum.

"It is, you know it is!" yelled Adam.

"They have to," insisted Mum desperately "They have to throw us out. It's the system. The Housing Office won't give us a home otherwise. Don't you see?" Adam choked back the tears. Mum looked at him firmly and then picked up the suitcase. She started walking towards the railway bridge.

"We've got to go and we've got to go now. They're expecting us up at the Homeless Unit. I've been there half the day already. But they need to see you and Lucy, just to make sure you're with Dad and me. Then they'll give us somewhere to stay for a while."

"Why just for a while?" asked Adam, walking quickly along beside her. "Why not for ever?"

"Because it won't be quite like a proper house," said Mum. "Look, it'll only be for a few weeks, or months — maybe. They'll probably put us in a B and B — a bed and breakfast place — you know, like a hotel. Can't be bad, eh?"

They walked in silence past the market and the underground station. Then they climbed the long, sloping street lined with shops and litter. They crossed the road near the top by the cinema. Then Mum stepped up into a narrow doorway with 'Council Offices — Homeless Unit' written above the door in gold lettering.

They squeezed past two rows of people and

struggled to one of the two thick glass windows that covered the front of the office.

"Oy!" said a woman behind them. "Where d'you think you're going, eh?"

"To get a place to stay," replied Mum. "They're expecting me to come back with the children, and then we'll get somewhere – they told me to."

The woman laughed, brushing her thick red hair from her face.

"They're expecting all of us," she said. "And they'll have to give the lot of us somewhere to stay before the office closes tonight. So you'll have to queue up like everyone else. Come on, come here behind me. Let the kids sit on the floor. There's nowhere else and it looks like we're in for a long wait."

Clutching their bags, Adam and Lucy sat on the floor, watching the scene in front of them. Occasionally they shuffled along a little as someone further up the line got their place to stay. But it was very slow. As people got served, they walked back past the two long queues, clutching a white card.

"Where are you going tonight?" the red-haired woman asked a young man and his son. The man looked at his card.

"Er . . . The Croft Hotel."

"Oh, that ain't too bad," said the woman. "They've just done out a games room for the kiddies. I know all these places – every one of them."

The man squeezed his small son's hand and went

silently out of the door as if in a daze. After a while another family queued up behind Adam and Lucy.

"Just look at all those children!" whispered Adam. There were seven of them. Their suntanned skin made them stick out among the pale faces of the people in the queue.

"Well, I reckon if they can afford a holiday, they can afford somewhere to live," said the red-haired woman.

The seven children were guided in a row by their father, who spoke to them very softly.

"Now just sit down there real quiet — like those two kids are, right?" He pointed to Adam and Lucy.

The man's voice was different. It made Mum turn towards the family.

"You're a long way from home," she said to them, smiling.

"Yes," said the children's mother, "thirteen thousand miles away! We're from Australia. But we decided to come here and look for work. Nothing much going on there at the moment, and I've got my sister over here."

"Where are you staying?" asked the red-haired woman, knowing now why they all had a suntan.

"On a campsite just outside the city," said the man.

"A campsite!" gasped Mum. "But it's freezing!"

"Yep," he replied, and then laughed a little. "Never really knew what cold was 'till I came here."

Just then a woman screamed and another started

shouting in the other queue. Adam watched in horror as
the two women kicked and punched each other. The
smaller woman pulled a fistful of hair from her enemy's
head. But the larger woman didn't seem to notice.

"No one," screamed the larger woman, "no one
takes my place in the queue — got it?"

And the brawl stopped as suddenly as it had
started. Through the thick office window, Adam could
see people working as usual. It was as if nothing had
happened. But he knew now why they hid behind the
glass.

Adam, Lucy and Mum waited another one and a
half hours before they got to the window. Two women
had pushed in front. But Mum couldn't bring herself to
say anything. The officer behind the window didn't
smile.

"Yes?" he asked.

Mum gave him a letter that she'd got from the
office that morning.

"That's to say we can get somewhere to stay . . .
and these are my children," she said quietly, pushing
Adam and Lucy gently forward.

It was early evening and dark by the time they
finally stood outside the Homeless Unit. Mum stopped
for a moment, lifted her head and breathed deeply several
times.

"Come on!" she said, sounding very determined.
"Let's go and find our next home."

They crossed the road and walked back down the

hill, aiming for the bright light of the underground station. In the station Mum stopped at a row of telephones to ring Dad at Kath and Chas's flat, so he'd know where to find them all. Then she bought some tickets.

Half an hour later, Mum and Adam struggled up some dark subway steps and into the orange street lighting.

"Come on!" shouted Adam to Lucy. She was way behind.

"I can't," she sobbed, "I'm too tired." And she slumped down on to the dirty stairs.

Mum dropped the suitcase and went down to pick her up.

"Don't worry," she said soothingly. "It's not far now, and I'll carry your bag for you."

They had to walk through a park to get to the hotel. The sleepy, leafless trees looked spooky in the lamplight. At the end of the park, a long, darkening street led towards a busy road. Mum stopped at the first tall building along it. Over the door, a large, blue sign with 'Parkside Hotel' on it creaked back and forth on shiny chains.

"Here we are," sighed Mum. "Come on, let's see what we've got."

The hotel was warm and smelled of food — all different kinds. A cheerful young woman rose from behind a desk in the hallway. Mum showed her the white card and a letter from the Homeless Unit. The woman nodded and unhooked a key from the green board behind her. She took Lucy's hand and led them all down some stairs into a dimly lit basement. They stopped at a door with the number 5 on it and the woman turned the key in the lock. Adam pushed his head around the door and stared.

The room was small, but clean. Two narrow beds were squashed together on one side, and a larger bed on the other. In one corner stood a washbasin. A dark wardrobe loomed near the tiny window that looked up on to the pavement. The middle of the room was filled with a round table and two chairs.

"You can do your cooking with the other families in the kitchen at the end of the hall," said the woman. "And there's a bathroom just opposite. Oh yes, and you have to be out of your room every morning between nine and eleven for the cleaners." She closed the door quietly as she left the room.

"Which is my bed?" asked Adam.

Mum looked quickly around her.

"It had better be the one near the basin," she said. "Lucy's bound to crack her head on it."

Adam pounced on a television set that stood on the floor near the big bed.

"Oh, great," he said, and reached for the plug. But in his hand he clutched only the frayed ends of wire, where someone had ripped the plug off. Adam looked up angrily at his mother.

"This isn't a home or a proper place to stay!" he

shouted. "You're a liar! This isn't anything at all!"

He flung open the door and ran into the hall.

Four

"Hi, there," said a voice from the shadowy stairway, "Where are you going?"

"Mind your own business. I'm just going, that's all," panted Adam angrily as he pushed past the small figure crouched on the steps.

"I bet you've got nowhere to go," the voice said calmly. Adam stopped suddenly and grabbed hold of the stair rail. "I HAVE! Don't you DARE say I haven't! Who do you think you are anyway . . ?"

"My name's Cal and if you had somewhere to live, you wouldn't be here," she insisted.

"Well just for your information, I've got an aunt and an uncle on the Bledlow Estate close to where our old house was, and an uncle who's got a farm in the country, and – "

"And nowhere of your own." Cal sighed and stood up to go. "And if you do go and stay with any of them, then you'll never get a place – you'll mess it up for your whole family."

Adam hesitated as Cal jumped the last three steps.

"Wait a minute!" Adam half shouted.

"Take my advice and stop being such a baby," said Cal. Then she pressed a button in the wall that turned a dim, frosted light on for a few minutes. Adam saw her thin face properly for the first time.

She said nothing as she opened the door to her room and then closed it again. Adam looked up quickly to make sure he could see the number before the hall light switched itself off again.

Throughout that night, Adam lay restless, snatching sleep between fits of crying babies and the click, clack of heels on the pavement above. A muffled alarm rang out at half past five in the morning. Another, closer and louder, buzzed at six o'clock. Their own clanked stubbornly from under Dad's pillow at a quarter to seven.

"Well," said Dad, "I won't bother setting the clock for tomorrow morning. There's more bells going off in this place than a ship in distress!"

"Who needs bells?" asked Mum. "I was awake half the night. Come on you two, it's a long way to school and Dad's got to go and see someone early, so let's get cracking."

"I'll go and make some tea and toast," said Dad.

"I thought this was a bed and breakfast place," said Adam. "You said they gave us breakfast in the dining room.

"We're too early," replied Mum. "We'll have to get our own."

"But you said . . ." insisted Adam.

"And I said get your clothes on," Dad told him firmly as he moved towards the door.

"What? With her watching?" Adam pointed at

his sister in disgust.

Lucy, too exhausted to fight back, just turned over in bed, covering her eyes with her soft cardigan.

"Good," said Adam, pulling on his socks and looking at his father with triumphant eyes.

In the still cold light, the family walked together through the park. Humped figures, covered with old blankets and pieces of cardboard, lay sleeping on park benches. At the other side of the park a young man with knotted hair and shabby clothes sat on the ground by the iron railings near the underground station. Close to him, a small black dog looked hopefully into his eyes. A scrap of paper with 'Please feed me' scrawled on it hung from a string round the dog's neck. Lucy put a coin in a woollen hat that lay open and empty beneath her feet.

That evening a very weary family returned to the cramped hotel room. While Mum and Dad waited patiently for some space in the kitchen to cook, Adam slipped out into the hallway. He walked towards the stairs and knocked very gently on a door to his right. A small, suspicious face appeared.

"Where've you been all day?" asked Cal, shutting the door quietly behind her.

"Our school, of course," replied Adam.

"What? All that way?" gasped Cal. "You must be mad!"

"Well we can't go to school here," said Adam. "Dad's asked for a new home near where we lived before. If we change schools now, we'll have to change back again. And that would be really stupid."

"It's really stupid you bother going at all," laughed Cal. "None of the kids here go, except two sisters in number ten, and that's because their dad's a teacher."

"A teacher!" gasped Adam. "Teachers can't be homeless!"

"Want a bet?" asked Cal. "His wife ran off to France and he couldn't pay for the house all by himself." She looked at him and laughed again. "There's all sorts here, you know."

"Where are your mum and dad looking for a house?" asked Adam.

"It's only my mum and me, and we're not asking for a house, just somewhere safe."

"Safe from what?" Adam sounded very bewildered.

"Safe from my dad, of course," Cal replied, rolling her eyes to the ceiling. "We've spent the last four years staying in different places. There was a really good refuge where Dad couldn't get at us, but it had to close down after the first year and a half. We got a flat after that, but he found us after a few months. So now we just move from one B and B to another."

"When will it stop?" asked Adam desperately.

Cal shrugged. "Who knows?" she said. "Mum can't get any work. People don't usually want you if you haven't got a proper address. They think you'll just move on . . ."

"Adam!" Yelled Dad. "'Your supper's ready! Come on, where are you?"

"I've got to go. Can you come out later?" asked Adam.

"I have to check my diary. I might be able to fit you in," Cal replied laughing.

Back in the room, Adam sat down at the small table, pushing Lucy's arm away from his table mat. He was determined to be even more difficult than usual. Cal's words had upset him and deep down inside he knew he blamed his parents for their predicament. Mum looked at him hard for a very long time.

"You know, Adam," she said finally, "we will have to be especially patient with each other in this cramped space."

Adam said nothing. He had always thought that problems like homelessness happened to other people, different people! They ate in silence, the traffic outside, the galloping footsteps and the clattering from the kitchen making up for their quietness.

Adam and Lucy learned to adapt to their new way of life in the hotel. They learned not to shout or to cry or laugh out loud, not to bang doors or block bathrooms, or run in the hallway or pound up the stairs. This code of quietness was unwritten and unspoken, but was kept by most people there. Only babies were allowed to break the rule of silence and cry when they wanted to.

In that small space, the family quickly found ways of living closely without snapping apart. Adam was allowed to change his clothes in the wardrobe, which Dad grandly called his dressing room! Adam let Lucy borrow his radio during the day. Like many children in the crowded hotel, Lucy often caught illnesses and had to stay there, moving from room to room when the cleaners came round in the mornings. Mum managed to cook their meals in one pot, sharing the kitchen stove with other mothers so that the children did not have to wait for their food at night.

But it was Cal who taught the children how to play. In the afternoons she met Adam and Lucy on the stairs as they came back from school. They all huddled together under the narrow basement window near Adam's bed, watching hundreds of feet go past. They counted them, then timed people as they strolled or scuttled from one end of the window to another. Lucy liked seeing how many different coloured shoes there were, or how many boots or trainers. Adam and Cal made up stories about the people who sometimes lingered in front of the window, waiting for friends or taxis. And in the evenings, when Lucy was in bed, Adam and Cal sat on the stairs, watching other families – trying to guess which of them would get a real home first.

Five

It was the weekend before Christmas. Adam and Lucy
had not visited Aunt Kath for a while. She and Uncle
Chas were getting used to their new baby boy, born just
a few weeks ago. Saturday mornings had been wet and
dreary ever since. But at last came one that was crisp
and clear, so Dad took Adam and Lucy to the park
nearby. The weak sun struggled to shine on trees that
were now a cold stone grey. Clumps of damp leaves had
been cleared from the paths, and the once bright flower
beds now lay hard and bare.

Lucy wove in and out of the trees, singing, "I can't
wait for Christmas, I can't wait for Christmas, I can't . . ."

"BELT UP!" screamed Adam.

"I can't wait for Christmas, I can't wait —"
continued Lucy in a high, squeaky voice.

Adam pounced on her, grabbing her coat and
shaking her until she started to cry. Dad pounded up to
them and held them both apart, one in each of his arms.

"Stop it! Just stop it! How dare you, Adam!" he
bellowed.

Adam struggled, banging his fists fiercely on Dad's
chest and kicking his legs. But Dad stood his ground
until his still strength finally tired Adam out. The long
silence between them was broken by Adam.

"She's just so stupid," he muttered.

"It's stupid to lose your temper in that way," said Dad. Adam knew he should say sorry, but he never liked doing that at the best of times. He looked up at Dad.

"I don't want Christmas. Don't let us have Christmas."

"I want Christmas, you selfish boy," said Lucy

"Why don't you want Christmas?" asked Dad.

"Because it won't be like it used to be. There's nowhere to put the tree. There's no money for presents. There's nowhere to play with toys even if we did get some," Adam blurted. "And anyway, I don't believe in stuff like that any more. Believing is just for rich people – people with a proper home of their own. It's easy to believe when you've got everything you want."

"Exactly," said Dad. "But who said that believing should be easy?"

Adam shrugged. "Christmas won't be happy, I just know it won't. And I hate pretending to be happy just because I feel I have to. Anyway, how are all those families going to cook their turkeys in just three ovens? We'll all be lining up until New Year!"

Dad looked at Adam's stubborn face and burst out laughing. He ruffled his son's hair and then hugged him tight.

"You're so practical!" he said. "That's your trouble. Just try and look for the little bits of magic in your life."

Dad carried on laughing all the way back to the hotel. For Adam, that was a little bit of magic in itself.

On Christmas Eve Lucy hung her stocking by the narrow window, certain that Father Christmas was going to squeeze through it.

"He'd better not," Adam had said, "or he'll land on my bed. And don't expect me to hang up a silly stocking. All I want are the things in my box at Aunt Kath's, and my bike and my skateboard at Uncle Ed's farm. I bet they're all rusted up by now, anyway."

But when the children were asleep, Mum hung a stocking for Adam next to Lucy's.

When the children woke that Christmas morning, they sat up in bed and stared in surprise. Lucy read aloud the frosted message on the window pane:

HAVE A MAGICAL CHRISTMAS!

Two red stockings bulged side by side. Coloured tinsel glittered around the table legs, the chairs, even the washbasin. Paper chains drooped like fishing nets across the ceiling and down the front of the dreary wardrobe. And on the table, for there was no other place to put it, a tiny tree sparkled with lights, and frosting on the tips of its branches.

"You see?" said Lucy, leaping out of bed. "You see, you see, you see."

Adam just put his head to one side and gave a little smile. He reached under the pillow and pulled out three small parcels, each one wrapped in kitchen foil and tied up with Lucy's hair ribbon. A picture of an aeroplane for Dad, made with matchsticks stuck on blue card, a brooch for Mum which he'd won in a school raffle, and a small wooden doll for Lucy.

There was no need for Adam to worry about a queue of turkeys. After a children's party early on Christmas Eve, most families had left the hotel to stay with friends or relations for a few days. The hotel was calm and peaceful.

"Just like Christmas should be," Lucy had said.

But their quiet Christmas was broken by a welcome surprise. Later that morning Uncle Chas came to fetch them in his van. For the first time in a long while Adam and Lucy went back to Aunt Kath's and Uncle Chas's flat, and for the first time, they saw their new baby cousin in his own home.

With crackers and party poppers on the balcony, this had to be the noisiest Christmas that the children had ever known. For Lucy, though, the best part was the baby, who made it what she called a 'proper' Christmas.

But Adam could not bring himself to look at his small cousin, nor to touch him. At the end of the day, he peeped around the door of the baby's room. A cot now stood where his bed had once been. A mobile of stars and moons twisted and turned where his Nighthawk had once swung gently from the ceiling. And in the corner a basket filled with bright baby's toys stood on top of his box of special things. A room of his own. Why should a baby so small have all that space to himself? Adam turned back towards the bright coloured lights that welcomed him from the sitting room wishing he had not been reminded of all the things he had lost.

Six

February was always the beginning of spring for Mum. No matter how grey and cold the weather was, for her, this was the start of new life. And it really was a very bitter Sunday when she rustled around the bottom of the wardrobe and brought out three old plastic seed trays and a small, half-used bag of compost.

"Where d'you get those from?" asked Adam.

"I brought them from our old house," said Mum.

"How come you had room for all that stuff when I wasn't allowed to bring my aeroplanes from Aunt Kath's?" demanded Adam.

Mum looked at him patiently.

"These were my special things," she said. "My only special things. But perhaps you don't think Dad and I should have brought any?"

Adam shrugged. He watched as she covered part of the window ledge with a plastic bag, laying the small trays side by side on top of it. She fetched a large spoon from the kitchen and carefully filled the trays with compost, smoothing her hand over each one. The first tray was filled with tomato seeds, the second with sweet peppers and the third with a mixture of flowers — promises of deep blue lobelia, stripy petunias and nasturtiums splashed with crimson and gold. Mum sprinkled some compost on top, patted it down lovingly, then watered the trays. Finally, she covered them with newspaper and stuck the bright seed packets into the edges with matchsticks.

"There!" said Mum triumphantly. "It's lovely and warm in here – those little plants will pop up in no time."

"But where will you put them when they're big?" asked Adam, looking at her as if she was mad.

"Well –" she began. "I've just got this feeling that we'll get somewhere to live just when they're ready to be planted out . . ."

"What?" asked Adam in excitement. "Did Dad go to the Housing Office on Friday and get us . . ."

Mum shook her head.

"Dad goes there every single day as you know, and one day we'll be lucky, but for now we just have to hope and try."

"Well I don't see the point," said Adam. "And I don't think we'll get any luck, either."

Adam went to school the next day feeling even more dejected than usual. The walk from the station to school led past the large housing estate where Aunt Kath and Uncle Chas lived. It was where they would get a flat too, if they were lucky. Lucky! Adam shook his head in disbelief. How could any intelligent person believe that this was a matter of luck?

He looked up at the tower blocks and scanned the windows. Yes, as usual, flat upon empty flat was

boarded up. Adam counted the ones he could see — ten, eleven, twelve — and far into the distance, council workmen were boarding up another one. So who were these for? Why couldn't they have one? He knew that Dad asked these same questions day in, day out. But he never got a reply. No one seemed to think that Dad deserved one. The family was powerless, and Adam felt the helplessness of it all so strongly that he wanted to burst. Adam's grim face was greeted by a smile from his teacher that morning.

"Cheer up," he said, "we're going to add to our project on our community today. You'll enjoy that, Adam — you're so good at making things."

Mr Bannerman turned to the class.

"I bet that some of your mums and dads are digging their gardens, ready for the spring," he began. "A lot of people have already started sowing seeds. So today, we're going to add gardens to the houses that we made last term. They'll be a bit bare for the moment, just as gardens are at this time of the year. But we'll add the flowers and vegetables in a couple of months' time.

"Don't worry if you've only got a balcony — you can use those small boxes on the table over there and stick them to the sides of the blocks of flats."

The children got down to it, and the sound of snipping and sticking soon filled the air. But Adam sat motionless, his head in his hands. Mr Bannerman came up and sat at the edge of Adam's table.

"What's the matter, Adam? Got no garden, eh?"

he said. Adam nodded, miserably.

"All we've got are three rotten seed trays that my mum put by the window in our hotel room," he said.

"Well, that's something," replied Mr Bannerman. "I haven't even got round to sowing mine yet. Come on, we'll find some small matchboxes for you to make your mum's seed trays with. She's trying really hard, isn't she? So you'll just have to try too!"

Adam made three tiny seed trays out of the boxes and filled them with brown tissue paper, to make it look like compost.

"And where shall we put your boxes, Adam?" asked Mr Bannerman.

Adam walked up to the miniature street and stretched over the houses and flats on the table. He reached right up to a large, white cloud on the painted sky.

"Here," he replied.

"Why there?" asked his teacher.

"Because my house doesn't exist," said Adam.

✦ ✦ ✦ ✦ ✦ ✦

Like the shock of a flash flood, spring burst open in the first week of May. It quite caught Adam by surprise as he walked through the park on his way to school. The sun hurt his eyes and the new green leaves were so clear he thought they would melt in the warmth of the morning.

"On a day like this," he said to himself, "something amazing ought to happen."

The day turned out to be exactly the same as every other school day, except that Adam had to carry his coat as well as his school bag on his way home that afternoon. The sun, the warm glow and the smiling people were just tricks. Adam was used to them by now, and stopped himself from being cast under their spell. Wrapping his thoughts up in a small box, he concentrated on what he would do when he got to the hotel room. But before they reached it, Mum guided them to a small museum on the far side of the park.

"Oh, no!" groaned Adam. "Not here again. We must have seen those manky stuffed animals at least ten times. Why can't we just play football in the park?"

"But I love the animals! And they're not all stuffed. What about the snakes and the chameleons?" protested Lucy.

"How can you possibly love them?" asked Adam. "Most of them are very, very dead and stiff, and they stare at you with spooky glass eyeballs – "

"That'll do, Adam," interrupted Mum. "We'll have a quick look round while we wait for Dad."

"Dad?" asked Adam. "He doesn't usually get back this early. Isn't he looking for work?"

"And isn't he allowed to have a break once in a while?" replied Mum with a smile as they climbed the stone steps to the museum.

Dragging his heels, Adam followed Mum and

Lucy round the dimly lit glass cases. The last case held two live chameleons. One sat on a stone, blinking its eyes and staring at the wall, its sagging throat throbbing in and out, in and out. The other one crawled slowly along a branch near the glass, climbing to nowhere, watching human creatures staring and then passing by. Seeing the chameleon moving round and round in that small space, its body almost disappearing against the dull brown branch, made Adam feel small and trapped, as he often did in the hotel room.

He shuddered and turned away, suddenly attracted by the daylight outside. He squinted in its brightness as he stood at the top of the steps. Then looking down he spotted Dad, sitting on the bottom step, staring into the park. Dad turned round and smiled at Adam, waving to Mum and Lucy as they came up behind. Slowly, he straightened his body and lifted his head.. He thrust his hand into a trouser pocket and pulled out a silvery key, which dangled from an old string.

"You've got a car?" asked Lucy in surprise.

Dad shook his head. Adam turned to Mum, whose whole face was smiling like a shining moon. Adam's mouth opened, but nothing came out. Then, stretching his arms out into a pair of wings, he hurled himself down the steps and ran round and round the sun-drenched park, shouting:

"A HOME OF OUR OWN! A HOME OF OUR OWN! A HOME OF OUR OWN . . . !"

Sitting together on a park bench, Adam heard how

Mum and Dad had known about the flat for a few days now, but Dad had wanted to get it ready for them with all their own things in it. Dad and Mum had spent two days cleaning up. The furniture had been brought over from Uncle Ed's farm in one of his trucks. Uncle Chas helped them to carry boxes from the flat, just a few blocks away from their new home. Adam and Lucy wanted to go there straight away

"Tomorrow," said Mum. "We've waited a long time, but one more day won't matter. Tomorrow we'll all go and live there for good. Anyway, we've got packing to do back in the hotel. But let's do it quietly and not get too excited, because so many people there are still waiting for a home."

"Some of them will probably never get one, either," said Adam, thinking of Cal.

Back in the room, Lucy started packing her things into a bag. Mum and Dad went to the kitchen to cook the evening meal. But Adam just sat by the washbasin, playing with his penknife.

"I thought you'd want to pack up quickly," said Lucy. "I thought you'd be excited."

"I am," replied Adam.

"Then you ought to be helping," Lucy snapped.

"I'm busy," said Adam. Holding the penknife, he bent his hand round the back of the washbasin and carved on the wall: 'Adam was here'.

"I'm going to tell on you," said Lucy.

"Why?" asked Adam.

"Because you've ruined the wall."

"So what? It's not our wall," muttered Adam.

"Exactly." said Lucy.

Later that evening, Adam strolled along the basement hallway and sat quietly next to Cal on the stairs.

"You're going," she said.

"Yep – how d'you know?"

"Your mum told me in the kitchen," replied Cal.

"Come and see us?" asked Adam.

"Don't be stupid," Cal said.

The two of them sat thinking their own thoughts, letting the stairway darken slowly as the light faded outside. After a while Adam drew his penknife out of his pocket.

"Here, have this," he said to Cal, pushing the knife into her hand.

"I don't take presents," she said, turning the smooth shape over and over in her fingers.

"It's lucky," Adam insisted.

"Idiot!" replied Cal, putting the knife in her pocket. Adam smiled in the darkness. Cal shifted up to the next step and put her hand on Adam's head, giving it a push.

"Go on then, shove off!" she said.

Adam crept down the stairs and turned round towards her, but he could not see her face properly in the dark. This shadowy figure, crouched on the steps, was how he would always remember her.

✦ ✦ ✦ ✦ ✦ ✦

Three weeks later, on the wettest June morning since records began, Adam burst into his classroom like a fireball from the sun. In his arms, wrapped in a dripping plastic bag, he clutched a long box.

"What's that, Adam?" asked Mr Bannerman.

"My new home — thought I'd make a model of it for our project," he replied. "Look! It's these windows here on the fourth floor, the ones with the yellow lights on. And look! I've done a balcony with Mum's flowers on them."

Mr Bannerman smiled.

"And does it still feel good to have a home of your own?" he asked.

Adam thought for a while.

"Oh yes . . ." he began. "I can be myself . . ." He thought again. "I feel like I belong somewhere," he said finally.

That evening the swollen grey clouds gave way to a glorious pink and purple sky. Lucy played on the balcony with a tiny ginger kitten. Devil could not live in a fourth floor flat, so with many tears Lucy had accepted the new pet, rescued by Adam from a tall, smelly bin. Mum was babysitting for Aunt Kath and Uncle Chas, so Adam was putting a box of toys next to his baby cousin, who sat propped up on cushions, well away from Mum's delicate plants. Dad thrust his head round the balcony door.

"Hello, you two — no, you three!" he said, suddenly seeing the baby.

"You four!" corrected Lucy, holding up her kitten.

"Found any work?" asked Adam.

"Nope, but I will. It's just a matter of time."

Adam walked towards the edge of the balcony and looked down on to the grass below. The pathways glowed with orange lamps. A shadowy figure looked up and waved at Adam.

"Watcha!" he yelled.

It was one of the Australian kids from that first frightening day of homelessness. The family had been given a home on the second floor in the same block. Adam shivered. Looking all around, he drank in the warmth of the lights radiating from homes far into the distance. He dipped his hand absentmindedly into his trouser pocket. But there was nothing there. He clutched the emptiness, and thought of Cal.

Organisations

Centrepoint
Central Office
Bewlay House
2 Swallow Place
London W1R 7AA
Tel: 0171 629 2299
*Centrepoint run a
'Leaving Home Project'
which aims to help young
people prepare for leaving
home.*

Child Line
Freepost 1111 London
N1 0BR
Tel: 0800 1111
*24-hour, free and
confidential advice line to
help children with a wide
range of issues. They will
listen, comfort and
protect.*

Citizen's Advice Bureau
Head Office
Myddleton House
115-123 Pentonville Road
London N1 9LZ
Tel: 0171 833 2181
*Offers free, impartial and
confidential advice.
Opening times may vary
and you may get an
answering machine.*

**National Federation of
Housing Associations**
175 Gray's Inn Road
London WC1X 8UX
Tel: 0171 278 6571
General information

*about housing
associations.*

The Samaritans
46 Marshall Street
London W1
Tel: 0171 734 2800
*Local branches are listed
on the inside back or
inside front cover of the
telephone directory. They
give emotional support
and are confidential and
non-judgemental.*

Shelter
88 Old Street
London EC1V 9HU
Tel: 0171 253 0202
*One of the main
organisations campaigning
for the rights of homeless
people and against bad
housing conditions.*

St Mungo House
Atlantic House
1 Rockley Road
London W14 0DJ
Tel: 0181 740 9968
*A charity which works
exclusively with single
people who are homeless.
They run several hostels
and support services.*

Social Services
Look them up under the
name of your local
authority in the telephone
directory.

AUSTRALIA

Shelter
Box 8
Trades Hall Buildings
4 Goulburn Street, Sydney
New South Wales 2000

**Youth Affairs Council
of Australia**
PO Box 108,
179 Barclay Street
St Kilda South 3182,
Victoria

NEW ZEALAND

**New Zealand Council
for Social Services**
PO Box 24 084
Wellington
Tel: 04 385 3358

**Auckland City Council
Youth Services**
PO Box 7107
Wellesley Street, Auckland
Tel: 09 379 8488
*Offers information on a
wide range of groups and
organisations*

SOUTH AFRICA

**Child Emergency
Service**
Tel: 08001 23321
*24-hour, free advice line
to help children with a
wide range of issues. Will
also refer you to other
relevant organisations.*

Books

Both Shelter and Centrepoint's Leaving Home Project produce a wide range of books, reports and videos on all aspects of homelessness (address and telephone numbers are given above).

FICTION FOR CHILDREN

Stone Cold by Robert Swindells (Puffin)

The Bed and Breakfast Star Children by Jacqueline Wilson (Yearling/Doubleday)

The Story of Tracy Beaker by Jacqueline Wilson (Yearling/Doubleday)

The Suitcase Kid by Jacqueline Wilson (Yearling/Doubleday)